K. E. A

LOSERS

Short Stories

161 Days

2019

First published in Poland in 2018 by Ridero

Translated by K. E. Adamus

Published by

161 Days

ISBN 9781912831142 Ebook

ISBN 9781912831159 Printed version

Table of Contents

SPACE SHITS

*W*hile sending application to university, Vlad pictured himself as a graduate differently to what have prepared for him reality. He saw himself as a forestry manager. But life follows its own rules, which should not surprise Vlad, but it did. He graduated as one of the best students, but his job applications were landing somewhere in the limbo and he never got any reply.

After six months, motivated by sarcastic statements of his parents, Vlad decided to apply for minor job positions.

He landed in the district of Dungs, as a simple forester.

Until now devoted supporter of living in peace with the nature, and a bit eco - freak, after one year of living in conditions of variable aura, he started to miss the consumer lifestyle. The leaking roof of his house during long November nights gave him a slight psychosis state. On that time, during first autumn spent in the woods, if someone would present his thoughts as a movie, even horror fans would flee from the cinema, where this film would be shown.

But the world did not know anything about Vlad and his thoughts, so the risk of being a subject of interest of a screenwriter was in this case low.

The only contact with the world was supplied by a landline, but only in rare moments between fights with the local poachers, who were probably educated in diversion somewhere in Libya. Most of the time the landline was not working. There were no signals in the forest, and his mobile phone was useless as well. His girlfriend escaped after first autumn flood. And no, it was not caused by a storm, but a small shower with cooperation with leaking roof, inherited with the house.

The moisture was everywhere. Vlad discovered a new type of mushrooms on the walls of his bedroom, but he was too depressed to share this discovery with the scientists.

During one year of living in the forester building, Vlad encountered several personality and mood disorders. First was neurosis, which evolved into psychotic sociopath's stupor, to end up with the local dungs' variant of depression.

At this stage the poachers were hunting next to his forester building, leaving active landline, as they did not need to fear any reaction from Vlad the forester. Vlad was sure, that this is the worst stage in his life. He even made up his own life philosophy, based on the content old, primary school newspaper. This philosophy could be summarized in eight points.

1. You will be a loser anyways, so there is no need to be proactive.

2. Even if you get any success, the fate and future is dark and stormy.

3. Do not be happy with what you've got, because other people got more of it.

4. Be worried in advance, so you won't be surprised with failure.

5. Spoil the mood of others - and you won't be alone in your grumpiness.

6. Be jealous about possessions of other people - you will be sad for longer.

7. The worst is your fate, the more you a liked by your friends.

8. The higher you get, the longer you will be falling down. And if you get too high, while falling, you will brake your legs.

At first Vlad wanted to share his life philosophy on Facebook, but he did not have access to the Internet in the woods. He could use a computer in the local library, but the librarian was a wife of one of the poachers, and some leftovers of pride did not allow Vlad to go there. After few weeks, Vlad added point number nine: "Life sucks if you can not think over point nine".

After few next days of summer floods in his house when he preferred to spend time outside, he did not have any problems to formulate point number ten: "It always can be worst".

This reflection was a result of finding purple shits in shape of gimlets, which he discovered in tree farm, and which burnt all the plantation.

After a year of strange experiences, the first suspects were the poachers. Vlad got really annoyed. This was really too much. These were his first emotions after long time of hebetude. Despite being angry, he was also scared of his boss' reaction, after getting know what happened with all trees plantation.

He spent few days at the computer, writing brief report, where he stated as the main issue purple shits. Caring about statistics, he went again to the plantation to count the dung. Unfortunately, during this time the nature was working as well, and all shits decayed. Vlad encountered another emotions - this time it was desperation and grief. He spent all day in the toilet, suffering with the diarrhoea. After his 15th visit he got an idea. He decided to make guilty all of the new spices of mushrooms, which were decorating walls of his bedroom. He ran to the computer to write down and print the report. He noticed, that there is no paper to print it. He decided to complete the report the next day and then buy the paper. Uplifted with his genius, he went sleep.

The next day Vlad woke up with empty head. He remembered, that he got some brilliant idea, but what was it? He forgot. Counting for other brilliant ideas he decided go for shopping to buy printing paper. He took with him three rolls of toilet paper, because the diarrhoea still remembered about him, and went to the shed to take the bicycle.

It was a self-made bicycle and war trophy, remembering times of his fight with the poachers. Awareness of having it in the shed was lifting up ego of Vlad - maybe he is not so complete of a loser? It appeared that he was. The poachers resigned from getting back it - the bicycle was too distinctive for further using. However, they decided, that Vlad will not use it as well. They distorted the wheels.

Vlad got angry again, and immediately rushed to the toilet. It pissed him off even more. He decided to go to the Dungs village on foot. His path was a railway track. It was straight line leading to the village. He just needed to turn in one place and he could reach his destination - the Dungs civilization.

Vlad walked through the railway track, getting off only when the rails were ringing, signalizing coming train or when he had another attack of diarrhoea. He did not want to die while making poo on the railway track.

"Maybe the depression is gone?" He analyzed these signs of precaution. During one sit under the bush, he was overtaken by a very fast locomotive.

Vlad experienced immediate gnosis. "What is going on?" He thought. "There are no that fast trains in this country. Maybe the poachers got a gift from Libia, after sharing stories about his failures?" He did not know, that he was overtaken by an alien with next door name X -442. The alien was banished from his planet because of bad football play. The emperor of his planet sent him to the Earth, were they were getting rid of trashes, putting them into bins, which were called by the people space ships.

The advisers of the harsh football supporter - The Emperor Y - ZXD, helped to find a destination country with the worst football league and that's how X-442 got to this country.

During first few days of his stay on the Earth he complicated life of few tax clerks and saved from failure many pupils, as it was time of exams, by hijacking a train from Dungs station.

What is interesting, none of the university students appeared on the station at this time, which could be explained by cosmic timing, acquired with surviving so many years as the adepts of this country scholar system.

K – 442 was hungry. He landed in Dungs' forests few days ago. Because of migration stress he got diarrhea, which imprisoned him in the area of forest chaos. His space shift was biodegradable, and was useless now. Nothing was linking him with the distant civilization where he was born and raised.

He appeared to be susceptible to Dungs' melancholy, but as a new in this ecosystem, he still had a will to fight. Unfortunately the melancholy lowered his efficiency, also the railway was not ready for someone more active, than the railway workers. Plus the locomotive was not steered with the thoughts.

The train derailed few yards after overtaking Vlad. X – 442 survived the disaster. He left the train and was forced again to confront with the chaos of the nature.

This time he found some civilization in shape of Vlad's house. He felt with his eighth sense, that there is no one inside. X-442 decided to look for something to eat. He did not know humans food, but liked the mushrooms in the forest, so he did not despise growths from the bedroom walls. An offensive smell from the toilet made him evacuate. While leaving he took with him a sporty longbow - Vlad's reminder of his student dolce vita life and activity in the student sport club.

In the meantime Vlad was walking to the Dungs village and decided to become an optimist and develop his ten points decalogue. After looking at it with an optimist's eyes, it was presenting like this:

1. You will be a loser anyways, so there is no need to be proactive, but you need to do something with your time.

2. Even if you get any success, the fate and future is dark and stormy, but at least something happens.

3. Do not be happy with what you've got, because other people got more of it, but they also have more troubles during removals.

4. Be worried in advance, so you won't be surprised with failure and furthermore, you will discover in yourself the skills of the prophet.

5. Spoil the mood of others - and you won't be alone in your grumpiness.

He left the fifth point unchanged, as a very optimistic one. He started giggle, imagining his own jokes. He just went out of the forest. There was an open space of fields, with shapes of poachers here and there, behind the wheels of their tractors.

Vlad felt, that another diarrhoea attack was coming. And he felt already the enemies eyes on him. He could not just go back to the forest. He made few steps, staring at the asphalt. Something of grey color appeared on the left side. He looked there. And the smile appeared on his face - first smile for months.

Along the road there was unnaturally deepened ditch. Freshly dug ground with a clay texture was raising sympathy of soil scientists towards the efforts of Dungs' farmers and understanding of their additional activity as poachers.

Vlad thought, that it looked like an activity of crazy man, who was afraid of the nuclear bomb attack and a big shockwave. This crazy man was a mayor. The elections were close, the asphalt was still good, which was kind of sensation, so he had to manifest his activity in different ways.

Vlad got in to the ditch and while making poo he started to think about point number six.

6. Be jealous about possessions of other people - you will be sad for longer, but at least you will have some emotions.

Encountering number seven, Vlad realized, he must do some logical mistake, because usually losers leave alone and nobody remember them. So he did not have problems to changing its formula.

7. The worst is your fate, the less friends you have and more time for yourself. Changing other points was easier:

8. Making no progress, you will not fall down.

9. Life is beautiful, if you can change all the points.

10. It always can be worst, but the most horrible shit can change into fairy tale.

Last affirmation was influenced by personal experience with end of diarrhoea. Still smiling, Vlad got off the ditch, only to fall back there, hit by a powerful gust of wind. His all clothes were covered in clay. Vlad looked at the sky. It was navy blue of colour and it started to rain.

Swearing horribly - his swears and curses were overheard by Dungs post office worker, and in shape of typescript were shared among poachers, causing a blush of shame at most rough men cheeks - Vlade get out from the ditch again.

He took a look around and noticed, that despite rain tragedy, his personal fairy tale still continue.

The poachers' tractors wheels were spinning. The machines were doing zigzags and were sinking in the mud.

Vlad watched this view for a while, then triumphantly he crossed the road next to his oppressors, sending them a look of Medusa, gained by too long stay in the forest backwoods.

This look was taken on the portrait photo to American visa, and influenced the negative reply about its issuing. Other reasons could be a fiery confession about love of nature and a desire to see all the wonders in the USA.

The trip to American embassy was the only day in the city since getting position of forester. Vlad was thinking about it. Suddenly he fell on uneven asphalt, fortunately on the other side of the hill, not seen by the venison enthusiasts. "Maybe I am a loser for everyone, but I like too much winning, to lose" He thought, contemplating a big mushroom next to his nose. "Mushrooms!"

Watched by a sneaky librarian he created a detailed report, writing about new spices of mushrooms, which contributed to the destruction of the forest nursery. He decided to send it by email. He lost trust to workers at the post office. He also checked his bank statement, which he was not doing since few months. He spent money only on food and hygiene, so the account balance was looking nice.

The diarrhoea gone. The rain stopped. Life for a moment became bearable.

Till the moment he went back to his hut and discovered that mushrooms are gone from the walls. Angry, he wanted to catch the bow and shoot his enemies pictures. But the bow disappeared as well.

Did the poachers plan to frame him in some bad deed? He should report the missing weapon. The landline was dead again. Before he will reach the village, the police station will be closed. This was enough. Enough of these permanent rains which conspired to fall over his foresters lodge. Enough of these dull faces of local people, watching, what, when and where is he doing something, just to poach whenever they want. No! He will not stay here anymore, even for more one second.

He caught his travel bag. Put there some underwear, clothes, passport and ID card. Nobody will notice his absence during few days. He can fly to Tenerife.

He could speak English and Spanish. Maybe he will find a waiter job, and will be walking between the tables, in the sun, for next few years, till he get promoted, or will earn for his own premise. And even if he won't find the job, he will rest for a few days. That's what he was thinking, rushing to catch the last train to a nearby city.

He did not know that his library visit and using the Internet, caused a wave of anxiety among the poachers. They decided to check their victim status, this forester - the loser. So the operation was successful, they drunk few litre of currant shine.

They did not predict one thing - the aliens are very possessive about their food.

The hungry alien just returned to the forester's lodge, after many forest adventures, thinking that mushrooms are renewable food and would fill his hunger.

One of the more brave poachers, Mr Smith, was just trying to check through the window, what is going on in the forester's house (Vlad left the light on, suggesting, that he is inside or will be right back). Suddenly the arrow shot his throat. The poachers froze in their positions. Oh, they did not suspect this!

Mr Smith was bleeding under the window, but no one went to help. Then they saw the alien. Each one of them thought, that the currant shine is guilty of these hallucinations. For sure this must be the forester, who went crazy, and dressed up like weirdo.

Mr Steven, who created currant shine, felt some responsibility. Quietly he raised his gun and aimed at the creature, who killed their friend. The alien was bending over the Mr Smith body. The shot smashed his head. An acid spilled out from the falling corps, spraying Mr Smith's body and dissolving it, while the owner was still alive. Mr Smith lost consciousness, and after few minutes his body stopped existing. Same as the body of far galaxy visitor.

The poachers, paralyzed, watched this scene. After few minutes the paralysis gone and they run away all at once. They run through the forest backwoods. Branches of the trees lashed their faces. Here and there one of them hit the tree. Mr Steven broke the ankle.

It's his house, where they were supposed to meet after successful operation. They arrived one by one, waiting for the owner to open the doors.

Mr Steven, supporting his body on stick, to avoid the pain, arrived after one and half an hour.

The loud debate started.

"We should report him to the police! There are dead bodies! There are no dead body! He's a killer!" The poachers shouted.

Mr Steven wanted to share with them gooseberry shine, but no one wanted to try it.

At dawn, three dare-devils decided to go to the forester's lodge again. They found some gunge at the place of crime.

The debate continued. "They need to tell something to the widow. Or maybe better not? She will not believe their story. And where is the real forester? Was he this creature?"

Vlad did not know anything about these incidents, basking in the sun and watching the beach sunbeds and swimming people. He was lucky and got the job.

After one week he wrote a short email, informing the boss about long depression time and fights with the poachers.

His successors could not believe in this. During their work they did not meet a single person in the forest. No one was picking up wild mushrooms or blueberries. When they were going shopping, all chats were silenced, and all people stared at them. It was stressful. Additionally, they could not find anyone to hire for forest jobs. This atmosphere made them want to escape from this place as soon as possible.

Among forestry students the legend was created about this place. Thought about getting this job made all students studying hard. All had excellent exams results. Vlad never get to know about his contribution to making students' life more tougher.

IS IT INCLUDED?

*M*y first day at the new work after a long period of unemployment. I passed the course; I completed the training. I thought that initially I will be doing some paperwork, but apparently, because of my charisma and good looks, my manager decided that today I will show a house to some old, single lady.

This house was an old hotel, which the old lady was planning to remake for rented apartments. I heard that the hotel was haunted. It has been advertised in our real estate agency for a few months and nobody was tempted to buy it.

I was a bit stressed, because of the big price of this property. Probably my "to be or not to be" in the company depended upon a successful transaction, as so far, I have not signed any contract of employment.

"Undoubtedly there is a mould now on the walls. You will need to cut off the electricity and show it in the darkness, like James last time!" Other workers noticed my stress and laughed.

"Oh really? So that's why the appointment is after dusk?" I was trying to be funny as well, but my mood was far from optimism.

At my lunch break, I decided to see the property one more time. "Forewarned is forearmed". I had already had the keys. It looked like I will not have time for the meal, but anyways I was too nervous to eat.

It was grey and cloudy. The house was also grey. In the windows sat the net curtains from before five-ten years before. I had a strange impression, that the house squats to surprise me with some forbidden ploy – for example, that suddenly the floor will break under my body, and there will be not only no transaction finalised but also I will land in the hospital with my leg in plaster for the next few months.

I had taken a deep breath a few times before I stepped on the stairs to the ground floor. A key did not match. Neither the first one nor the others. Did I get a wrong set of keys? Maybe it is a joke on the novice and all today's presentation is a wind-up? Maybe they wanted me to come here at 6 p.m. and get a heart attack when the keys won't fit? Or maybe they know about my mental health problems and are making fun of me?

In high dudgeon, I jumped into the car. Two flashes from the speed cameras on the way back to the office certified my anxiety.

"Very funny!" I wanted to control the tone of my voice while throwing the set of keys on the manager's desk.

"I do not understand." He answered.

"The keys do not match."

"How is it possible? How do you know?" The manager's amazement seemed to be real. Or maybe he was a good actor?

I described the situation and my investigation of the property before the planned appointment.

"Are you sure that the keys do not match? I was opening this door two weeks ago…" The manager was checking keys, looking at me like a half-wit.

"I have a degree so I know how to use stupid keys" I answered, probably not necessary mentioning about my education, which at this post was useless. Plus, I have not mentioned it before in my CV.

"I will send there Barbara" The manager decided.

I was sweating out waiting for the return of my colleague. Maybe indeed I can not open the door? Maybe there is some gimmick there, for example, you need to pull in some direction the handle in shaped like a human palm? By the way, who installs such handles in the hotel? Nothing unusual in it, that they become bankrupt. Or maybe this is my strange, kinetic hallucination?

Barbara came back with a mysterious face. She confirmed my side of the story. The keys do not match.

The calm and lazy atmosphere in the office has changed immediately. Suddenly everywhere flew papers and curses. The manager took all sets of keys and drove to check if there was a mistake. There was no mistake. None of the keys matched.

The manager made a phone call to the owner of the property, asking if he resigned from the sale and changed all locks.

"No, I did not do that. But it lasts too long. Maybe I will let the sale to a different agency" Said the owner.

We started a hunt for a locksmith. Nobody has investigated further why the keys do not match. They had to fit at 06:00 p.m. when the old lady will come to see the estate. None of the locksmiths wanted to take this job, explaining this by saying it was a haunted place, bad luck or too much of other work. I got remember my friend, who had a few charges for burglary. Nowadays he was working as a handyman. I recommended him to the manager. My friend was finishing work at 05:00 p.m. and he could come to change the lock at 05:30 p.m. I was sweating in my suit. Will he manage to change the lock on time? I decided to focus on my presentation, not to get anxious thinking about possible bad situations.

"This old hotel is brilliant for remaking a block of apartments, which will provide a permanent income in the amount of…"

"From this side, there are lovely views on the La Manche canal, and from this side to the town, and from this one to the hills…"

One more time I memorized all the advantages of the building. Walking distance to the train and bus stations; in the town centre, but located on the quiet street. I had to admit, this place would be nice to live in, but I felt some antipathy to the building, which could decide about my career as a real estate agent.

My old friend came on time. We were sweeping the scobs when the old lady arrived. That time we could enter the property. The manager took my friend and went away, not to make a crowd. I stayed one-to-one with the client.

I started the presentation of the property, showing the ground floor, where there was still left a reception desk and a bar for the guests.

The furniture was old. I was going to mention it, but when I looked at the wrinkled face of the old lady, who was staring at my legs, I gave up on stressing the age of the objects.

I was showing one room after another. The client was just nodding and stayed silent, making no comments. It started to make me confused a little.

On the second floor, I felt a strong smell of male cosmetics. There was a steam coming from the open door of the bathroom.

I felt a bump in my throat and I lost both thread of conversation and my voice.

The old lady revived and took a look inside first.

"Is he included?" She asked.

In the bath, covered in strategic places with foam, there was laying a young man with a mohawk hairstyle. He had a muscular and tanned body.

"I'm so sorry, I just made here a small squat. Yes, I am included."

"I am buying this property! Walking distance to the town centre, this is it! Do you have an agreement?" The woman asked me.

As far as I knew, the agreement should be signed in the office. I just had a copy with me to show it in case of any client's doubts. I handed it to the old lady. She signed it and reached out a hand.

"The keys!" She said.

The sale finalization took usually longer than five minutes. I was hesitating. To give her the keys or to call the manager or even to advice not to make so fast decision? The last thing probably I should not do in this kind of work.

"Give her the keys," said the punk man from the bath. "You will not sell this property anyways. I live here for two years, so I know what I am saying. "

In case, he was just my hallucination, I ignored him.

But I handed keys to the lady.

Our office was already closed. I called the manager and I summarized the course of the presentation, not mentioning about squatter issue.

"Have you seen my son?" The manager asked.

"No, I have not been yet introduced to your son" I answered with diplomacy.

"You have not seen the punk in the bath? He saw you. You know, in this kind of work we have to do many kinds of tricks, otherwise, we would not sell anything. But do not tell the other workers."

Did I mishear him? Maybe I had not recovered properly and started to work too early?

I could not sleep the whole night. The next day I had two other appointments and I was not sure, what awaits me.

ME AND MY ENEMY

$\mathcal{F}$or a long time I couldn't get used to weekly visits. At first I missed them; I waited for them with longing. Later, fear appeared, because the priest explained to me that I was meeting my greatest enemy. Each meeting was accompanied by different emotions. I watched her face, which with each meeting became more and more washed out of emotion and I had mixed feelings. Is it really my enemy? I felt pity, not hatred. How did it all start? From shopaholism? She took me shopping. Each store has a different smell, different music, different decor. I felt important when I bought more and more unnecessary items. They gave me short-term joy, a fleeting impression that life for a moment had become better. For example, clothes. I touched the fabrics and imagined the touch of his hands. Will he like it? Rough woolen sweaters and jeans fell off. What about colours? He liked white and hated grey. And I would meekly buy white clothes, persuaded by her. Sometimes dressed in white, I felt like a grotesque swan or ballerina who ran away from the stage in the middle of the show. O! I had such escapes under control, and she always helped me.

'Why continue college and be a student of poverty?' she asked.

At first I resisted her whispers. At the end I admitted that she was right. I quit my studies and went to work. Three years of practice and I had my own beauty salon open. So she was right. I could buy white clothes that excited him so much. It doesn't matter that I had to squeeze the blackheads out of my clients and inhale the smell of their sawn nails. I had their praise as a sweetheart. How beautiful and young I look, what a great partner I have, how wonderful my life is. She used to sit in the back sometimes and tease me about it.

'Nothing can help the one with the pimples. Even after the antibiotics you advised her to take, she'll still be ugly. She wanted her fingernails orange again - the disco is playing! Why did you propose this super procedure to the third one? Don't you know she fancies your husband?"

The last one was the strongest. I felt like I was suffocating and left the facility for fresh air. I inhaled clouds of exhaust fumes from a busy street.

'This is such a good place to open the place,' she said few years ago.

The worst part is, she was always right. Five months passed and my husband started buying white clothes for this otter. And he never bought me anything, saying he didn't know anything about it.

'He got bored. Everyone will get bored. Do you have anything wise to say? Maybe if you'd finished your studies and started reading more, you'd have matched that otter. She has graduated from law school. And you've only had a high-school.'

'It was your idea to quit college!" I interrupted her monologue. She didn't like it very much.

'Do I interrupt you when you say something?'

'No, because you never let me get to the word.'

'As if you had something clever to say', she said and shattered the door.

My husband had left, my shopaholism had left. She didn't leave. She advised me to get rid of these horrible white clothes. I did too. I wanted to buy new ones in vivid colours. But I didn't feel like parading around in red or yellow. I bought five gray shirts, five black sweaters and five navy blue pairs of jeans. Black underwear. When I saw white inserts in nice clothes, I was going crazy. Sometimes I would destroy them in the fitting room, but only in the shops, where the shopkeepers could not monitor the quantity of clothes I tried on.

'Will you be a minimalist?' She joked.

Sometimes I enjoyed her sense of humor. Then I decided that it wasn't joke, but a very good idea. I started to explore the principles of this difficult art. After white clothes, it was time for things bought together with my ex. I threw them away like crazy until the rooms and walls were almost empty. At first I felt better, then anxiety came. She stopped giving me advice, I decided to do it myself. All these problems - it certainly had to have something to do with my inner self. I enrolled in a meditation course, it was so fashionable. I laughed at the activities with my clients. I came back from classes with a good humor. 'You often chat about this young meditation teacher' she said.

I turned my attention.

'He is supposed to belong to this cult, you know, those who live in these old factory buildings ' I laughed at them further away.

'There must be a lot of women there,' she summed up.

That one sentence made me crazy. How does he dare to smile at me? I spoke out of the next lesson.

'It's not true what people are saying. Come and see,' he said.

'Stop attend the classes' she advised.

I listened to her as usual. I accidentally met him in the grocery store. He looked so attractive and smiled at me.

'Don't listen to her,' he said. 'She is your enemy.'

'Is it possible?'

'Our priest will explain everything. A very clever man, he has a PhD in psychology. He will help you in this separation. First you will see her every week, then every month. And finally you will forget about her. Did she ever come in handy? How would you live your life if she wasn't there?'

'It's some cheap psychoanalysis,' I said, and I returned to my life.

It wasn't the same anymore. I remembered the heat waves when he looked at me. I was explaining to myself that after all, it's hot and humid. After a few months I saw him in the winter. A known heat wave flooded me. He advised me to find another spiritual mentor.

'You've learned a lot from me. Time to go through the next class.'

I decided to meet with the priest.

'She is always one step ahead. She is a toxic person. You won't be happy to be friends with her. When you have little money, she will advise you on a crazy purchase on credit. When you're rich, she'll say that you don't deserve anything expensive,' the priest explained.

Everything was right. How could I not see it? Despite this, I defended her obstinately.

'We're not talking about material goods and shopping, that's over. Now the problem is spirituality.'

'Do you suffer when you hear her opinions? Does she care about your well-being or does she torment you with every triviality?'

We were sitting in a café. I was afraid to go to an old factory. There were various stories about the people who lived there. When I saw a priest, I had the impression that I had known him for many years and that he was a good friend of mine. He didn't judge, he didn't bother me as much as she did. He had an answer to everything. And most importantly, everything that he said about me and her, was correct. I was afraid that he would spoil the nice atmosphere and start talking about some exotic god whose name I wouldn't even be able to repeat. However, he asked about me. It's been so long since anyone talked to me about me. The clients always wanted to be in the centre of attention. They described their weddings, breakups, secret meetings with lovers, difficulties in raising children. Sometimes I deliberately mixed the components of the masks in such a way as to stiffen facial muscles and discourage monologues. Rarely did she ask me how I was doing, how was my last day. And she? She assumed that she knew very well what was best for me.

She was able to explain everything so logically that every time I believed that her solution was the only option. The priest really knew me. He was like an expert on souls and guessed what was in mine. He knew me better than I knew myself. I drank green tea and thanked him for the meeting. I probably won't meet him again, but he explained to me many things. I wondered how to talk to her about this matter. If she is really my enemy, should I open up and discuss it with her? What if she uses it against me? She knew so much about me. In her case, however, I wasn't happy about it. She didn't have such a warm approach to me as the priest. Days passed. She talked about the need to earn money and save money for later.

'Take overtime, take on these extra clients.'

And I, as usual, listened to her. I worked for fourteen hours each and was physically unable to spend the money I had earned. When I finished work, the shops were closed a long time ago. Online shopping? The bright light on the monitor was striking and tiring. I slowly turned into a robot. All the activities were done automatically. She helped me for the first time.

'You've gone into a dead end, take one day off.'

I took two. On the first day I slept. On the second day I decided to cook a homemade dinner. I had enough of the ordered takeaway meals. I met a teacher and a priest in the grocery store. They greeted me like an unseen friend for a long time. They were asking questions about everyday life.

'You are tired,' the priest noticed. 'We just built a small spa in our buildings. How about a few hours?'

I went. These people were so fantastic! Everyone had a lot of talents. I believed that I had them, too.

Life in the factory was interesting. We painted pictures that we later sold on the Internet. We wrote poems. We prayed and meditated. As I was told earlier, I could see her every week. At the beginning I carefully prepared myself for these meetings. I dripped in oils and salts and put on colourful robes. However, I was forbidden to do so. So when I saw her every week in the mirror brought to my room, her face was getting grayer and more tired. More and more greasy hair strings.

'The enemy!' The priest screamed.

I rarely answered, trying to remember every detail of her face or mine. Is it true that our appearance is only a delusion? That our desires and emotions are only hostile whispers, and their lack is the nirvana we should strive for? In a week's time I see her again. And then there will be visits every month. But it is my enemy, the priest cannot be wrong. It was her advice that caused all the trouble. I am not in danger here. Nobody will give me stupid ideas. I'll be better off without her, for sure.

THE SELLER

*H*is company's dress code allowed him to wear clothes manifesting his mood. Unfortunately, he could not allow himself any sufferance grime or other expressions of a man who was depressed.

Jack had to smile.

After the last border control, he knew that the quality of his smile was poor. During the procedure of comparing Jack's face with the passport picture, Jack tried the best door-to-door seller's smile. As a result, the officer checked the passport in detail using some proper vetting. That was why people did not want to buy his books, examples of which he was currently carrying in his black shoulder bag.

Jack was toiling step by step through the slushy berm, execrating at the absent council members. Why had they not made a proper pavement? He was swearing at his old PE teacher as well, because he wanted pupils to jump over the puddles on the way to school, instead of sidestepping them in a cowardly manner.

Jack did not want to sidestep the puddles, not saying about jumping above them. He was floundering through the brown water not noticing that it slopped to his left shoe through a small hole in the sole. He finally noticed this, and thinking about all these marks he would leave on peasant's carpets made him happy.

"Man! Who has time for reading books nowadays?" That's how they were putting off his florid declamations – those fine spun sentences, which were created during sleepless nights.

Not quilted, the grey coat did not protect him against the cold. But the worst were the dogs.

Village barkers' manners in the post-communist villages are different from city curs, walked by the distinguished old ladies. The biggest ambition of the village dogs was to pluck the turn-ups of the door-to-door seller's trousers. Especially, the turn-ups of the door-to door seller who suffered from depression.

Jack was surmising, that even in the act of lenity or stupidity, he would sponsor an anti-aggression therapy with a proper dog's coach – he would lose all the money.

In reality, he had to spend that money on another pair of black trousers. Bigger dogs were barking lazily from the inland of backyards, on chains linked to dog houses. Smaller barkers were enjoying freedom, and were using it to get rid of their inferiority complex.

The village was called Dungs.

Even if he would not have known this name, Jack would have known that he had been screwed and left in a deep septic tank.

The company was day by day becoming more and more similar to a cult. Each month, the workers were transported to different parts of Poland.

From the morning till late afternoon, they would try to palm goods off to the incredulous residents of towns and villages.

After work, they would gather in the hotel. The company covered the costs of accommodation. Each seller who has earnt more than fifty zloty during the day had to bang the gong. They would take it to every new place they went. This gong played the main role in Jack's nightmares, if he managed to fall asleep. The main role in these dreams had a murder weapon. The victim was their manager, who was conducting a proper brain wash for them every evening in disguise of effective sales training.

In the beginning, the unfolded visions of high income and good career made Jack an optimist. But soon, the brutal reality and horrible weather brought his common sense back.

Looking ahead objectively, he was aware of the lost position. His peers were making careers in international companies and were at the end of paying back their mortgages.

Jack had no power to dream that one day he would become the owner of a real estate or even a car. So far, the other sellers were giving him a lift. Jack was not a yuppie. He changed his unemployment fate for the grotesqueness of a cold caller job. In the beginning, he tried to get used to his new life and role, trying to expound himself that orthopaedic pillows would straighten peasant's hunches and curvatures, and that juicers would add vitamins to their organisms, whose main feed was potato, and that the books would evolve an abstract thinking in a tractor driver's mind. The feeling of the mission flying by dawned on him, as he stood face to face with a potential client.

"Sorry, I don't need your pillow. Tesco got even better." The town people were saying.

"The best pillows are down pillows" He heard from the village people - in cities they got all artificial stuff.

"First of all you need to make the client feel that our product is necessary in his life" Effused Marc, the manager, during long evenings. After lectures, he tested their knowledge about formulas, which the sellers were supposed to use to brain wash clients.

Jack always stuttered with words "offer of the life time", which annoyed the manager. Jack had a weak memory – he preferred to call it selective – and he pleaded this fact during the explanations.

This argument did not satisfy Marc.

"A child in kindergarten would memorise this text faster! And you are working for us for three months."

To be accurate, after ten weeks Jack took some days off, excusing himself by a difficult family situation, and he went to London to look for a more normal occupation.

Unfortunately, English people could not understand his fluent English and they put him off by talking a lot about financial crisis in Europe. Maybe, if he had more time for seeking employment, his fate would have changed. For example, he would have worked as a kitchen porter or would have been cleaning London's streets.

Failure escalated the bitterness that Jack could regard as his only foregoing life legacy. In desperation, he tried to take a loan and go to France to look for work there. He did not know the language of Paris residents.

But he faced the fact, uplifted with the knowledge of his compatriots' relations, who were going abroad without any knowledge of languages, and he believed that there was a method in this madness. But there was a catch in Jack's madness. The bankers found those catches fast. One of them was the lack of a permanent income.

"There is a very big demand for orthopaedic pillows in our society" Jack tried to unroll visions of his prosperity.

That moment, when it appeared that a would-be client was insolvent, the smiles on the bank workers' faces disappeared, and in their place, grim- faces emerged.

Before he left the bank, Jack cursed at all bank staff in his thoughts. Like a proper loser.

"Good bye!" He said loudly, trying to slam the door, which was another failure, as these were revolving doors.

The memories of his failures were fuelling Jack's melancholy while he was walking through the village. He was watching houses' yards steadily trying to figure out, where it was worth to enter, and which places were better to forget. The livestock in the yards in the shape of dogs, giving high level signs of being alive, was a big "no" and a disqualification for the house. Thereby Jack was breaking the rules of his company and his boss Marc to enter each single house. But he did not want to waste time.

This day so far, he had managed to sell only one book, bought by an old grandma, probably because of the greediness to just have it and the lack of any shops in a few miles' area. In more favourable conditions, this old lady would probably have become a shopaholic.

The house number 219 had a very well kept front garden. Whoever was designing it knew his work well. Feeling a trace of civilisation and prosperity, Jack pushed the garden gates. He rang a doorbell. After a while, a door opened, and from the inside, there blurted a smell of cooked dinner. He could not feel anything traditional and this seemed to him a bit suspicious. Even more suspicious was the natural hair colour of the woman, who was standing at the door. These were not good signs.

"Good afternoon, madam!" Ignoring these fatal signs, the seller started his standard formula. "I am representing a Marketpol company. Do you have a while?"

"It depends for what…"

"We are doing some market research about reading habits in this village. Could you please answer a few questions?"

"Yes. I can talk about books. Please get inside."

"Entering the house is half of success" Thought Jack, remembering his boss' words.

"Would you like some tea?" The woman asked.

"Yes, please."

After a while, he received a cup of tea with some oriental aroma. Jack started considering if it was ok to swallow the anti-depressant pill in the presence of client. Usually he took it a few hours before the general meeting with Marc, allowing the medicine to start working at the proper time. "So, what is your research about?" The woman interrupted his divagations. Jack took out from his bag, a special survey, and started reading the questions.

"How often do you read books?"

"I read around three books per week. Mainly the Nobel prize winners' books. Our library is well-equipped. But the Clancy is next to Camus, and "The Vatican cellars" are between the books on religious studies. Well, I try not to complain."

"Ah! Nobel prize winners" Said Jack, regretting, that he did not swallow his pill. Now he could not do this, as looking for the medicine in his bag during the chat would be highly impolite.

He started asking other questions, losing faith in selling his stock of books with every answer that he received. But after completing a survey, he said the eternal formula about the "incredible offer" and took out few romance books, encyclopaedias, and a Polish epic book.

The woman looked at them and took "A small encyclopaedia of reptiles" in her hand.

"This should be useful." She said. "You know, the bricklayers make few fudges and the floor is not even. I need something nice to put under one desk's leg. And this book…I can even read it…"

In this way, Jack earned another five zloty. He also attained the library address. It was based in a school building with a separate entrance. He went there and entered into the midst of a storm.

"I have not borrowed this book!" A young blonde in an animal pattern coat was shouting.

"The card is on your account." Answered the librarian.

"But I have not borrowed it. Do I look like a chicken raising fan?"

"We can't do anything. You will be able to borrow books next, but first, you need to return "Chicken raising" "Answered the librarian. "What can I do for you?" She asked Jack.

He solemnly showed her the books and started to talk about the "great offer". His words did not impress the librarian, but when she saw the colourful covers of the romance books, her eyes started to shine.

"I will go to ask my manager" She said, leaving the room.

The consultation must have been successful, because when she came back, she bought ten books.

On the street, the blonde amateur of raising chicken was waiting, cursing at the mess in the library. She bought three books.

Jack did not listen to her, being with his thoughts in the hotel. He had earned seventy-five zloty today. It was his first success in door to door selling. Walking to a place of meeting with his motorised colleague, he started deliberately thinking about his achievement. Firstly, it was optimistic, but the depression was stronger. Tomorrow will be another uncertain day. Losing his optimism, he reached the bus stop. Victor arrived after twenty minutes. He was not smoking any cigarette, which meant that he had a bad day. They drove in silence to the hotel.

At the reception, Jack collected his parcel with betel nuts. It was a gift for Marc the manager, who was a fan of all kinds of nuts. Jack had chosen this gift after getting information that betel nuts made the teeth black. Jack read this information in one of the books he was selling.

After a small lunch, all sellers gathered in the conference room. Jack rang the gong. All sellers looked at him and started saying congratulatory words with fake smiles.

"Well, well!" Commented Marc. "Looks like we have a new sales leader!" Using the temporary interest of the manager, Jack gave him a packet with nuts.

"What is it? A bribe?"

"It is a drug." Answered Jack. "It has similar qualities as nicotine. " "A drug is not a bribe." Said Marc and took a packet fast. "So! We are ready to start?" He shouted.

All sellers took their places at the conference table.

"Today we are going to memorise the types of clients." Marc started talking. "Who remembers the types of clients?"

"Those who know that they need the product, and those who do not know this yet" Answered Victor, playing with a packet of cigarettes.

"He had a bad day, I have not seen him smoking today.." Whispered a few persons.

"Yes, that's correct.." Continued Marc. "We like the first type of clients the most, but I am telling you – the client, who gets to know that he needs the product is an even better client."

The sellers started whispering and commenting quietly.

"So, how do we convince a client, that he needs a product?" Asked Marc. He opened the packet and started biting the nuts.

"We say about the qualities of product!" "We say that the neighbour had bought it!" "We inform them about its purpose!" All sellers started shouting out answers.

The manager nodded, intensively chewing nuts.

"But what is the most important?" He asked after a while.

The silence begun. All sellers were thinking intensively, pursing their foreheads and trying to find out a satisfactory reply. Some were not thinking, waiting for the answers of others.

Marc was watching all of them, eating another betel nut. "The most important is demonstration!" He said after a while.

Suddenly his eyes blurred. The packet fell from his hand. From the throat of the manager a deep strange sound came. He fell on his knees.

"Is it a new technique?' Asked one of the sellers. "The client will buy it?" Asked another.

The manager fell over his side. Through his half closed eyes, they could see only the whiteness. From his mouth, a small stream of saliva came out.

In the sudden silence, they could hear only the spluttering of the manager.

"I think we should call the ambulance .." Said one of the sellers after a while, but nobody reached his phone.

"I will call." Victor said. "I already have had a bad day. "

While Victor was calling, all sellers gathered around the manager. "It is strange" said Nick "He is lying in a so called safe position."

"The safe position looks different!" A few other persons started arguing. The sellers started a debate about how to make the body of the manager safe. Everyone after the first aid course had different suggestions, but nobody touched Marc.

Breathing equally as heavily as the unconscious manager was Jack. He had a strange impression that he had not read the information about the nuts till the end. He started thinking of removing the packet but was afraid that later it would be described by the police as an act of removing crime proofs.

After an hour, the ambulance arrived. Marc was taken to the hospital, where he died a few hours later.

In this time, Jack already knew that too much of betel nuts could cause death.

At dawn, the new manager arrived.

"Death will not destroy our success!" He said during the short meeting. Jack did not listen. He was thinking about his own cruelty during childhood, all this throwing out of flies' legs, and concluded that now was the time to pay for these crimes. In the meantime, a pathologist discovered a new toxic substance in the dead body of Marc. The investigation started slowly. After a few weeks, all sellers received letters with police appointments.

Jack, at this day, got diarrhoea and spent half of the day in the toilet. On the day he got arrested, it was raining.

"It was a joke" Jack was trying to convince the policemen.

"Do you have any mental problems" Asked one of the policemen.

"Yes."

The psychiatrist was bald and tired. "Do you hear any voices?" He asked.

Suddenly Jack felt that the gate was opening before him, and he entered it.

"Yes" He answered. "I can hear voices."

A BET

*A*ndrew was fumbling with the shirt's buttons. He never could fasten them properly. They were so small. But the shirt looked very smart. And a good look in this game is like a pillar.

"Are you sure, you took out all the money?" He asked, looking at Maggie. When she nodded, he turned around towards the mirror.

"You have nothing to say, as always." She read his lips.

Could she make a mistake? Did he say something different? Maybe she is oversensitive? No, it is not possible. She had never made a mistake. She was paid for lips reading. She passed millions of tests and has never made any single mistake.

She was stressed. Illegal bets could damage her career. Plus, Andrew was not winning for a long time. Maybe today will change everything? Maybe Andrew is nervous and that's why he said so?

"Calm down" – she wrote on a piece of paper. Two years of being together, and he still does not want to learn a sign language. Why? He wrote back "Do not screw up" and then he left.

Maggie was still sitting on the sofa. Finally, she had proof that something was wrong with Andrew's attitude. A proof, that he does not love her anymore. But maybe… Maybe it was just a vision of the game and the bet, which changed him for a while? No. She was suspecting him for lack of feelings since long time. And now she had a proof.

She decided to buck up. She had to visit a stakeholder. Chess was not so popular among the gamblers, but today was also a football match. If she won't go out in ten minutes, she will be late.

Maggie came up to the mirror to check her look. Were the signs of disappointment visible? Or any signs of uncertainty? No. She looked beautiful, as always. Involuntarily she took a look at the picture in frames. Maggie as a regional miss of beauty. Unfortunately, among disabled women. But maybe she was deaf without speech, not to get above herself and become lofty? It's enough of these thoughts. She smartened her modest, black cardigan up.

On her way she made a decision. She will go to the real stakeholder. This illegal one was always cheating with the percentage of won money. Well, mainly these were Andrew extra money, from his unregistered work, but also all her savings. She won't give it to some defraudant's hands.

And maybe Andrew will calm down, when he will see a doubled money? She wanted to convince herself at the same time calling herself an idiot. She has eyes, she can see, that it is over. Yes, they live together, but she means nothing to him.

At the stakeholder, she understood why Andrew sent her somewhere else. The maximum bet amount was only 70 pounds. Will she manage to place a bet on time? She ran out and sent a text message to a familiar taxi company, the only one who agreed to send a cab after receiving text message. Unfortunately, everything got also a dark side. She could order a taxi this way, but all cabs were late…

She took a place in a second row. The tournament did not begin yet. All players were eyeing a young Russian, who was new to them. As Maggie knew from written by Andrew's notes, the Russian player was a wild card to them. All players knew already their own strategies and tricks, but they had no opportunity to work this Russian player out.

Andrew watched few videos from new player's past tournaments, but the young man seemed to have no habits. His was playing passive till the first mistake of his rival. Then he attacked. And was winning.

Maggie was waiting for Andrew to notice her, to give him a sign, that she has done her job. But he was flirting with his manager. Very disappointed, she started to watch other players. Everyone behaved unnaturally, pretending relaxed; laughing loudly and clapping their rivals' shoulders. Maggie looked at the Russian. He was staring at her and sent her a wink. A bit ashamed, the woman turned her head in different direction. Could he know her secret? No, probably she is oversensitive.

The tournament started half an hour late. Andrew won two first clashes. In the next one his rival was young Russian.

Maggie could not see the chessboard, but it looked like Andrew was not doing well. He unbuttoned his jacket and loosened a tie. Instead to watch the rival's moves, Andrew was watching the manager. Only when Russian made a move and pressed the chess clock, Andrew was trying to see and focus, what has happened on the chessboard. Of course, the Russian won. Andrew seemed to be surprised. He was so sure, that he will win all the tournament.

"As a tree surgeon you are better?" Maggie read the lips of Andrew's manager. She could not see his lips, but she judged from gestures, that he was arguing with the woman.

He turned back to Maggie suddenly. "I lost! Are you happy?"

All people started look at her like a brimstone, who forbid to play chess, wants him to make a real job and so on. And it was not true. In real, she was encouraging

Andrew to take part in another tournament. She was boasting his successes in her work.

"We are coming back!" Decided Andrew.

He did not say a single "I'm sorry" for lost money. Maggie was thinking, how to start this touchy topic.

Back in the house Andrew started an open war.

"Why you are not talking at all?" – He wrote on the piece of paper.

Maggie all bubbled up, when she answered in sign language: "Because I put all money on Russian".

Andrew got angry.

"You know I do not understand anything from this! That's enough. I'm moving out. Maybe I will find a normal woman."

Maggie took out a big suitcase and started pack his things.

The illegal stakeholder has cheated this time as well, but there was one third more money. She could start her own business. But the money was nothing, comparing to the feeling, that she put on Andrew's rival. Maybe she was not such a complete loser?

THE CHRONICLER

*O*h, how demanding my lord is! Not enough, that chronicles I have to write, but still into buffoon to change it is needed in the evenings.

Ribald jokes, rhyming, to wisecrack. The bawdier, the guests are happier. Ah, those guests! If not armors, and their helmets, undoubtedly their brain would run far away! behind the fields of our town. Nudges I often get, sometimes also offers I hear by no means humble, always then, when outfit womanly I wear. Of God they are not afraid!

The castle of the lord gloomy is. Already long time ago I would have died from torment, if not my dear Hermenegilda. Lord's sister's handmaid she is German, in captivity kidnapped. Her face common", is brightening only on my view. Ah! Why I so little these pages have stolen, there will not be enough space, to describe the grace of this maiden.

Cold winds came earlier this year. The sun we have not seen already for three weeks. Gathered ravens and crows on the fields. Bad it is omen. There is not enough of mind already to think up poems. I am rehearsing similar songs, when the men drunk are already, but to mislead their ear I cannot. What my fate will be, when into disgrace I will fall.

Hermenegilda for help for my mind from newts the skin is throwing out and an elixir to make is intending.

But enemies on the castle has many, among them Jagusia, who elixir of youth to obtain wanted.

First glimmers smattered a pile, and I thought that my heart will break. Hermenegilda, what have you done? Pale her face. Is looking at me with her bright eyes.

'Rhymes offer, buffoon!' requests my lord. 'But speedily!'

As a man not feeling quite, a poem sad in honour of my Hermenegilda to create I want, but swords of gentlemen nearby, and a smell of smoke reminds me, that mortal just I am.

Is burning my Hermenegilda!

Gentlemen and ladies are sneering at my stanzsas, and my beautiful witch's heart is breaking. I am stripping her of dignity, making fun of her uglinesses and ruin.

"A witch love wanted

In a fire of a pile she enamored"

I am declaiming these and other stanzas. Smell of the burning body attracted black birds. They are waiting for their feast.

Wealthy are laughing till their sides ache. And I am sad and tears I am holding back.

"He who betrayed the black heart

With the black feather his hands will embellish

And when down the feathers blood will flow

Human figure into oblivion will go away

Will mourn for me at the end

When the night of his will become day"

Sang my Hermenegilda. Throng froze. Ladies closed their mighty gobs out of fear, gentlemen took the swords.

'Vile plague, you will not scare us!' cried out brother of the lord and threw the sword at my darling.

The weapon pierced the body of Hermenegilda. She died in double tortures, from the fire and the sword wound.

Everyone dispersed quickly, and I by the lord called, next stanzas shaming witchcraft had to invent. Additional pages to the chronicle I received, to describe in it the bravado of my lord against powers impure. About his great courage I was just writing, when suddenly something black flashed in my eyes. I am looking, and here the feathers black from my hands are growing. Not much time passed, into black bird I turned.

Thoughts of my own, the body unfamiliar. Scared greatly, that someone will see me in this condition, out of the window I flown to the roof of the castle.

And so already moons many have been passing, as into the black bird I turn, when I take the goose feather to my hand. The chronicle to write I have to everyday. The courage of the lord there beautifully described is, and for me each time scary it becomes, what will from this whole tragedy arise. The death I am not afraid of, but my Hermenegilda I would like to see again. And where now she is, in which afterlives her soul is wandering? I would like to explain her the lack of my bravery, but yet any excuse I have not found.

Into black bird I turn for a half of the candle burnout time. I circle above the castle, and other birds feeling outlandish blood, attack me. I disappear fast in my chamber before they come after me, but dread tremendous is hounding me, if someone will not see me in condition like this.

The love to the witch cursed is. The heart of mine yet is beating for her, but why would I faithful to her remain? A marriage we did not take, as a water holy would burn her skin. Oh, my Hermenegilda, why did you the soul to devil give away?

And Jagusia more and more beautiful to me seems to be. The eyes of her like green of leaves, are sparkling to me, when she is laughing at my comedies. The hair of her black and in the curls. Often into the bird turned I sit in the window of her chamber, when she is trimming a cloth and other feminine tasks doing. Innocently my darling is looking.

I am cursing the witchcraft of Hermenegilda. With stamp of her passion she marked me for the eternity probably whole. What did mislead me, to do with the witch little love dalliances? Spell and charm assuredly she casted on me devilish, let her vanish in hell.

Into disgrace of the lord undoubtedly I fell. He told to read me his glory from the cards of the chronicle and dissatisfied through chambers is walking. The idea of Hermenegilda to my memory I recalled and I am afraid to execute it. In her intention a description of the lord with dragons fighting to include into chronical I should. But will this not be a blasphemy? And maybe of a witchcraft they will accuse?

More and more clever poems I invent at night and next day during a feast I declaim. For a court life for me there is not enough time.

But I am updated with its history. As the black bird I sit in the windows and I listen to the human conversations. Myself a human already undoubtedly not being. Be cursed, Hermenegilda and be cursed your devil's heart. Why have you done it to me? God made you a woman gentle, devil vindictive.

The poems of mine boring to the men already seem to be. Rarely a laugh already to provoke I am able. And once got me drunk my lord, of the buffoon wanting to make fun, rather than of his poems. When my brain was bemused, dangerous stories about black birds to narrate I started, until with a goatskin showered I became and bumps many I got.

I was sent to my chamber. I grabbed a pen, wanting in the chronicle the truth about the lord to reveal and his emblem of a hare heart. Soon into the bird I turned. The blood, either of a human or from impure forces, was buzzing in my head. To the window of Jagusia I flew over.

And she there with the lord is frolicking. The hands of him in the curls and on her waist are roving. A squawk terrible from my throat got out.

The lord got afraid, as he, and having heard my stories about the black birds a destruction bringing.

Already the whole court is hunting me, and to fly further I am afraid of, as soon the half of the candle will burn out. An arrow of the brother of my lord, the same who with sword hurt Hermenegilda, hit me in the left wing. I disappeared behind the tower and hardly to the chamber of mine I reached.

Now I am sitting with the wounded wing. Initially with fear was bothering me the thought, what will happen, when into human turned again, the wound I will have on the left arm. But the candle is going out almost, and I am the anger of the witch discovering right now.

"And when down the feathers blood will flow
Human figure into oblivion will go away"

O cursed my fate, of a luckless chronicler. The foreign glory to describe I had to, in the foreign chambers to live. But human it was given to me to be.

The devilish witch having the curse thrown, permanently me now into a raven turned. And abject my fate, as her was.

The door of the chamber is opening. An adjutant of the lord of mine to entertainment of evening to call me came.

He is crossing himself on my view. The candle already for a long time is smoldering. I will not wait already for the human figure.

Not considering the wounded wing, I am soaring into air and flying through the window. Other birds are sleeping, as the night already black has fallen. I am flying as far as possible from the castle, cursing the brother of my lord. Maybe if he with sword the menial wench did not strike, a next stanza she would give, how from trouble to get away I should. Because she was not bad, this my Hermenegilda.

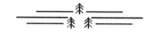

BIOLOGY LESSON

*M*y brain was functioning better than my peers, so throughout primary and secondary school I was convinced of my genius and the inevitable bright future that awaited me in my adult life. One would expect it to end up digging ditches. The fate was more sophisticated. I was mowing grass in ditches. Every day at seven in the morning I got on a special lawnmower and slowly covered kilometers, putting the civilization order in place of the chaotic nature. Marek, who accompanied me, burned out the salary at that time, inhaling smelly cigarettes. I, on the other hand, was thinking about Canada. It is said that the roads there have a specific, pebble-like structure, requiring regular hardening by means of a road cylinder. This machine moves even slower than my lawnmower. I felt a special brotherhood with a Canadian worker who was operating the machine. I suspected that it was an adventurous experience. On the other hand, he might have thought that working on a lawnmower in a post-communist country also had to provide an unusual experience. Of course, if you knew about the existence of Poland. I did not experience any adventures. I even complained about the stagnation and pain in my ass.

I was getting to the mowers hitchhiking. I diversified the drivers' journey by complaining.

I can confidently say that I am a champion in this field. This time I was getting ready to tell the story of the previous day. Here it is. I thought I would die of a stroke after two smoked cigarettes. The tides and currents of blood in my brain really were a good morning story. The Mercedes stopped. I boldly opened the door.

'Good morning! You' re driving...'

'Get in! What a meeting!'

It was Zenek. In order to describe Zenek, I have to go back to the lessons in basic science and biology. We learned about Zenek that he does not swim in the river because he is afraid of crocodiles. On another lesson he was picked up by policemen. The reason was that he put the logs on the tracks. Zenek never saw a train derail and wanted to see it with his own eyes. I learned about myself that I am so talented and intelligent that I have a guaranteed success in every field that I decide to explore. I was now standing insecure, stepping from one shoe to another, stumbling on suspiciously at panels in Zenek's car.

'Get in, get in, get in.'

I got in. I forgot about my future death and remained silent. Zenek was the first one to make a conversation.

'Going to work?'

'Yes.'

'Where do you work?'

'I am mowing the ditches' I whispered.

'Are you kidding me?' He was surprised. 'I thought you were going to college.'

'I was studying.'

'What subject?'

'Ethnology.'

'Aah! It's something about butterflies!' He got amused.

I didn't have the strength to confront the mistake.

'But mowing ditches after college? Life sucks' he continued.

For the sake of accuracy, Zenek only finished the basic education. I was relieved when I saw the lawnmower. Zenek suggested that we go out for a drink sometime. I agreed that the idea was good and I quickly went out of the car. Marek was already there.

'Will you smoke?' He pulled out a pack of cigarettes towards me.

DAY IN XXL SIZE

*D*espite the lack of cooperation from the receptionist, Nina managed to sign in to the sports center just before 11:00 am. She started to review the classes' schedule. At this time, class about the mysterious name "spin" began. It's probably some aerobics. Judging by the name, probably quite demanding and with rapid sequence of movements. All the better. She will burn more calories. In the second room there was a "bootcamp", but it certainly was not for her meager possibilities.

She sought out the building where she was supposed to sweat and tire. Remembering home-made workouts, she wondered if she was able to spend a full hour on exercises. The receptionist in the building with a lazy move scanned her new membership card.

"You're lucky" she said. "We already have only the last two spots to take classes. The best is to sign up two weeks in advance."

"Rat race! Everywhere this rat race!" Thought Nina, and she said loudly:

„I will try my best!

"Can you sign up right away?"

"I do not know how I work ...I'll come back ..."

"You can always let us know if you cannot exercise..."

In this way, Nina signed up for a "spin" for the two upcoming weeks.

The room was easy to find. You could hear from far distance loud music and fast tunes. Those who dared to take class with such rhythms certainly got proper sweat!

In the corridor outside the room, both women and men were crowding into one wall, leaving half of the corridor free.

Nina said "Hi", but noone answered. Only the woman nearest her smiled, but quickly the smile gone, as if the woman forgot that she had any reason to smile and fell into her thoughts.

"She probably thinks what she will eat for supper!" Thought Nina.

Only three people talked to each other, commenting on the dirty sports shoes of one of them.

"There was the mud! - explained the owner of dirty shoes.

"Where?" Her interlocutor was surprised. "It rained three days ago ..."

Nina looked at her tattered footwear. These shoes were already a year old and began to rub lightly over the toes. And the rest of Nina's clothing did not look good either compared to others. She put on an old, gray and loose (yet) tracksuit and a navy blue T-shirt from Primark.

"I'm sweating and I will sweat even more! Why would I wear a better T-shirt? It's probably understandable that I put on old clothes ... "thought Nina.

Others wore branded clothes, one set of which probably cost a quarter of her salary. But Daria also wore chic clothes. With her low pocket money, there must have been a way to get them cheaper. She will have to ask her daughter.

While waiting for the class, Nina felt an adrenaline rush and got memories of old trainings from the past. Judo classes at the first year of uni. She was even good until she injured her knee in the mountains, lifting a heavy backpack. There was also such an atmosphere before classes. Electric currents in the air. The slight nervousness of the training participants - they did not stand in the queue for cash, they just waited for the taugh workout and sweat.

Nina remembered how she always managed well and optimistically entered the hall with others. The room was not big. Two opposite walls were lined with mirrors. Nina looked at her reflection. Damn it! Is she really so fat? Something must be wrong with these mirrors. After all, even in shop windows, she looked better. Perhaps it was the right time to give her beloved, slimming mirror to Daria and buy such, which would reflect her true image?

People began to set up rows of bicycles, crammed far under one of the walls.

Nina liked the bike at the gym, she also liked a regular bike, although the last time she was riding it was about ten years ago ... But classes with bicycles? She once saw a movie that frozen her lazy spirit. The coach gave a proper workout to the bikers. It looked like pure pain, sweat and tears. No, she will not cry.

Unconvinced, she pulled out her bike as well. Suddenly she thought of her poor knees, which had suffered some injuries. There was no chance she could stand the pace. What to do? She looked around the room. Everyone carried their bikes with liveliness. Nina quickly put the bike back in its place and escaped.

Until late in the evening, she was haunted by the look of a guy in the hall who was watching her efforts to put away her bicycle. And the receptionist's face ... Well. He will send them an email later and will cancel all classes. Such a disgraceful escape was not encouraging. It is difficult to have a weak character. And excuses about weak knees will not change that.

But in the end it was not so bad. She went to the gym room and practiced with her tortoise pace for forty minutes. She also cursed herself that she indicated in the form that she knew how to use machines. These strange constructions certainly could give her some fame on YouTube if someone spied and filmed how she was going to use them. Just in case, she used those that looked fairly simple, though, to be more confident, she carefully studied the pictures with instructions on the machines.

"A diet day scored or a diet day failed? - Two hours later Nina was biting a pen, brought from the reception desk, staring at her calendar. All right. By half day she ate only 600 calories and then half a pizza. That's about 1600 calories. Total of 2200? She reached for the calculator. This is some kind of failure. She can't count so simple equation, and she once had a good score in math at high school. Maybe it's the fat that slows down thinking. Or maybe her brain is sabotaging the tracking of results and distracting the other side of the brain so that she doesn't think so much about her failure today? The calorie limit set by a dietician was 1500 calories. That is, only 700 calories surplus. She was at the gym and burned about 300 calories. There were 400 left and a total of 1900 calories were burnt. That is, a normal dose of calories for a hard-working woman. She had a sitting job. But it was hard work. Very hard. So should she score or not score?

"Don't cheat!" - she thought and put a big minus with red gel-pen at the bottom of the calendar page, with the words "follow a diet".

Nina imagined the noise of pouring Coca-Cola into a glass. Billions of bubbles, the clatter of ice cubes. She pulled another sip of water with disgust. Who thought that this liquid was healthy? It is not tasty or colourful. The nutritionist did speak in superlatives about drinking this liquid, but she had a cardboard box of fruit juice on her table, which she tried to hide after encountering Nina's gaze. And what is going to disappear from this drinking of water? A few pounds and cellulite? Rather than drinking water, the hump will grow on her back, like on the camel. What is worse, hump or cellulite? Nina threw herself into the cupboard. Surely there should be another can of Coke.   She   looked through her notes from the last weeks. The longest she managed to follow a diet was three days in a row. And then she was buying pizza. This was caused by a mad attack of hunger or an impulse, triggering a whole series of disastrous moves - a vision of pizza, a vision of the taste of pizza and a vision of satisfaction with pizza. Do they add drugs to the cake, making it so attractive? One has to think about it all.

If she manages to endure two or three days, and then a crisis comes, she has to prepare for it, like a faithful one waiting for the coming of the Messiah. Clog the fridge with healthy food. Block the telephone numbers of all pizzerias within a few kilometers. Prepare in advance some food, so that there is no excuse, that she is tired and does not want to cook anything and that she does not manage to do it on time, because she will starve to death.

To eat small meals every two or three hours. Alternatively, add an extra portion every third day - it is better to eat 400 calories more than 2000 more.

But what will she do with the other half of the pizza? Does she have enough willpower to throw it away? She used to mask it with something and put it in the fridge. The next day, after being heated in the oven, the pizza tasted just as good. Sometimes Daria noticed the presence of forbidden food. 'What is it?' She was screaming from the kitchen at the time. 'You will never lose weight! Why do you talk to motivate yourself when you cheat! You are fooling yourself and me! You cheat yourself more than you cheat on me, but you cheat on me too. In total, you cheat on two people. Or even three. Because maybe you are also cheating on your future boyfriend. Maybe he exists somewhere and your character suits him. It would be a so-called soul relationship, two halves and so on. But he wants the other half to be thin. And you are the only one who is the „other half". You are the only one in the whole world. So you are also cheating on him. That's three people now. And you're also cheating on this wise friend of yours. I heard you talking a moment ago and saying that you hadn't eaten pizza for two weeks. And you eat every two days...'

'Every four days,' said Nina.

'...That's four people...'

'Don't theatrize the situation.' - she cut off conversation because she was afraid of further ranting, which hit sensitive points. "Theatricalization of the situation" silenced Daria, who usually breathed furiously at the time, slammed the door of the fridge and then the door of her room.

Nina knew she shouldn't talk to her daughter like that. Only by accident did she find out about her professional plans. Daria never told her about them. And even her father knew about them. He called as soon as he got acquainted with their only child's plans.

'Do you think that if I work in a bank, I can give loans to everyone?' He roared furiously to the phone.

Nina let herself be provoked. If it weren't the common child and single motherhood, she would also be making a career now.

'Yes, Mr. Banker, send us some money, because we're out of toilet paper, and the money from the banker is only worth enough to be wiped off with...'

'You'd even accept it in such a state!'

Nina disconnected. In a moment she got a text message from him: "Tell Daria that she won't get any loans."

Nina's first thought was that Daria was in debt. But as for her age, she was a sensible girl. So if not debts, what? Drugs? She looked too healthy. She smoked cigarettes - as a former smoker, Nina was sensitive to smell - but that's where it ended, she guessed. Maybe. Nina felt hungry thinking about the problems with her adolescent daughter. She decided to withstand the attack of cravings and went to a nearby supermarket. Here, however, her strong will was lost.

Nina escaped from the shop alley, where salads, spinach and all kinds of fruit and vegetables were on display. Everyone there was so skinny and too healthy. Not yet today. O! Here is her kingdom. And there you go, promotion. For something she hasn't eaten yet. After all, you have to try new things in life, and not eat lettuce all the time. Who survived on lettuce? Dinosaurs certainly not. And she has no intention of sharing their fate. There you go. Orange bars in chocolate. Chocolate mini bars. After all, you have to make changes gradually, don't you? You can't just root them out during one visit to the vegetable department. But she has a way of doing it. She sneaked past the alleys, but seeing a nice saleswoman who praised her healthy food choices yesterday, she headed for the self-service cash desk. There will be no witnesses of her failure.

Unfortunately, the cash register spitted out half the money and refused to accept the banknote with which she wanted to bribe the machinery.

'There are always problems with this machine!' The saleswoman immediately showed up at the flashing cash register and with a few efficient moves, she tamed her. She looked into Nina's basket and with a blink of an eye, she said, 'Enjoy!'

Nina's enthusiasm, ignited by the vision of a new sweets, faded. She took the bars into a disposable bag and dragged herself home. But not all is lost. She found a way to satisfy her desires. With an efficient movement, trained on thousands of chocolates, she opened the package with ten orange bars. It smelled. Bitter chocolate, orange and some spice. Nina's hand trembled. But no, she will not eat any of them. She will trick herself and hide them in the corners. And then she will forget. And if she remembers them, she won't find them anymore. After all, this always happened when she found a new hiding place for keys, glasses or mail. The first bar goes to the coin drawer. Who else could keep the coins in the drawer? She pulled out the coins, looking for bigger denominations. A packet of cigarettes leaned out of the coins.

'I got you!' she almost screamed.

So this is where Daria keeps her cigarettes. She pulled out the cigarettes and opened the packaging. Only three inside. She put the pack back. She will not make a scene to the daughter. It is much better to control the amount of cigarettes flowing through the drawer for some time. She will know how much Daria smokes and whether it's an addiction or just a so-called smoking problem. It's time for her to fight. She won't condemn her daughter if she is in the clutches of a food addiction herself.

Where to hide the goddamn bars? She' ll find them everywhere. She will come here at night and will find them in the dark. Even in her dreams, sleepwalking. Nina sat down on the floor and felt sorry for herself. What did she do to herself? Are these candy bars worth it? She unfolded a piece of paper that smelled of cacao. It would have tasted good if it hadn't been provided with tears flowing down Nina's cheeks. She ate these goddamn bars, sobbing. Soon the nose started to leak.

She decided to get up. But it turned out that it wasn't that easy. It would be simpler in Nina's version by twenty kilograms slimmer. Resigned, she fell on her knees and in this way she managed to get to a chair where she had a handbag with handkerchiefs. Always, but not this time. This time she changed her purse before leaving, but she didn't put the handkerchiefs in it. She gave up, rubbed her nose with a hand sticky of chocolate.

That's how her former husband, who's got into the kitchen with Darya, saw her 'You have the feeling! You haven't seen me yet and you're making a scene!'

'Hello, sir' Nina tried to maintain strong, but she wasn't very convincing. 'Mom! You're eating again! What is it? You said you'd make a salad for dinner!' 'There were skinny cunts crowding around the lettuce!'

'One of them was probably my girlfriend, was she a size 10, a white dress and long blonde hair?'

'Yes, someone from the grocery store suits you' Nina took a revange.

.Argue, but I'm only giving you ten minutes, because I have important news about my bright future' said Daria.

'Well, you're going to study law, aren't you? Don't I know anything about it? What's the new news? Did your mother turn you into a humanities student so that you could continue the family' traditions at the reception desk?'

'It is better than... ' Nina cut it off. She won't argue in front of Daria. She better not learn pathology.

'You can't even finish a sentence?'

'I'm going to be an actress!' Daria screamed.

'And I'm having a date!' - Nina answered.

She was going to cancel the meeting, she didn't need it, but the presence of her ex-husband and the disloyalty of her daughter, who told him about her plans, did their job.

An hour later, Nina was walking around the canteen at the bus station. Through the window one could see people eating unhealthy sandwiches. The scent of garlic could be smelled. Oh, she'd love to eat a garlic sauce sandwich now. Only she would smell like garlic. And the jacket kept on the buttons so on faith. If she had eaten something, she wouldn't have fastened it. How come all the party clothes are too small? Did they shrink in the laundry?

She stealthily looked at her reflection in the window. It didn't look good. Thick legs in fashionable skinny jeans. A flattened belly. And also red boots, despite the nice weather. Unfortunately, it was only these shoes that she stuck herself in. The rest of the shoes didn't want to get on swollen feet. Well. Guys don't know anything about fashion. He will probably notice nothing. And where is he? It's been fifteen minutes since the agreed time...

She checked the phone in her hand. It was set to vibrate, so that she could feel it when message comes or when someone calls. Someone. In the profile photo he looked average. But she's not Miss Uniwersum either. The problem is that he doesn't know what she looks like.

She gave him her weight. He made a joke, that he doesn't know about pounds, because he's used to giving weight in pounds. And that he likes curvy girls.

They even talked on Skype. She
turned off. He said she had a nice voi‹
meet right away, but Nina said she ha
she would save some time and lose weight. Sh‹ ...
thinking she would lose weight in two weeks? Probably
she read too many women's magazines at the reception
desk.

He offered to come and cook her soup. After this
soup, the disease will surely pass.

She has already been waiting in this place for forty
minutes. Fortunately, people changed when they got on
the buses, so there were few witnesses to her waiting.
Apparently, the fate of Cinderella, who was late for the
ball, was not written to her. Neither were the shoes too
big. She contemplated for a moment her feet and calves
in tethered boots. She barely fastened them. And what if
the zipper breaks down?

'Nina?' she heard behind her back.

It was him. He was average-looking, but with a nice
smile on his face. She tried to smile. She saw his smile
slowly fading and turning into a grimace of
disappointment. After all, she told him she was fat.

'How was your journey?' She asked.

She had this question prepared in advance to begin the conversation. She knew that in strategic moments she sometimes turns into a mute.

'What kind of journey?'

'Well... Here...'

'Ah, there were traffic jams... How do you feel?'

The conversation didn't go well. He was clearly leading the conversation out of politeness. Insulted by this fact, she answered in half-worded words. Let him suffer.

'Coffee?' He asked.

Yes, he did. Now it's coffee. And when they talked, he wanted to meet at her house. Probably in the well known purpose. And what? He went through it? After all, she doesn't look that bad...

'Coffee? 'He repeated.

She agreed and led to the most expensive café in the city. Let him suffer. He will suffer even more, because at least an hour he will have to spend with her by courtesy. It's good for him. Surely she will not make the situation any easier for him.

'So how do you feel?' He talked to her again.

She didn't answer. In silence they reached the café. The smell of panini could be felt from inside. It is better not to go inside, because she will order three portions and will be embarrassed. She saw a free table outside the café.

'I'll take places!' she rushed, squeezing herself to the table.

She sat on a chair. Only now did she realize that she doesn't know what they're going to talk about. About the weather? It's hard, she'll survive this hour somehow. Apparently, he wasn't in a hurry to chat, either. A couple of minutes passed, and he was still buying the damn coffee. Suddenly she saw him. With impetus he left the café and quickly walked away towards the bus station, taking out his phone and calling somewhere. Did something happen? She heard the vibrations in her purse. It was him.

She saw him move away and called her.

'Hello?' She answered the call.

'I'm sorry, I can't. This is too much.'

Nina disconnected. So this is it? Even by courtesy he didn't want to stay with her? Or maybe coffee is too expensive? Actually, it's good. She won't have to look at the grimaces on his face. She felt as if she was watching the whole situation from the side. The whole incident was strangely indifferent to her. And that was the only thing that moved her. Something must be wrong with her. A normal woman would start cursing, crying or would catch a bastard and beat him with a bag full of cosmetics accessories inside. So that he could feel all the powders, creams and correctors on his grim face. And what about her?

She acted so calmly, as if she deserved something like that from life. She stood up quietly from the table and moved towards home. She was tempted by the smells of food from numerous restaurants and kebab shops. But she decided that only at home she would order something for takeaway. For example, a pizza with mozzarella cheese baked in the edges. She had her own idea for a pizza. She always ordered with mushrooms, pineapple, olives and sometimes branded herbs. She will eat the whole thing.

The phone vibrated . It was him.

'I'm really sorry. I'm calling to tell you that I've blocked you on all the portals and on the phone, so don't send me any messages...'

Nina hung up. What an asshole! Where do they come from?

"Someday I'll laugh at it!" she thought and felt better. Maybe karma will kill the asshole and he will choke with his soup. Or he'll have gonorrhea. Second phone call. That's the boss this time. Emergency, will she go to work today? Nina reluctantly agreed. Two hours later she was sitting at the reception desk. "God, how terrible that light is..." - Nina thought, "Don't complain, woman." She hardly took off the bracelet from her thick wrist and put it on her other arm. It was Ludmilla who offered her this exercise. A month without complaining. And if she gets caught whining, she has to move the bracelet from one hand to the other.

"God, my hands are so fat!" Nina sighed.

She put the bracelet back. Yes, it was better now. The other hand is probably thicker. And so every time she caught herself complaining and put the bracelet on, she had to complain again because her left hand was swollen and the bracelet after a few minutes of wearing caused pain. Because of this she probably developed a habit of whining, worse than if she hadn't been paying. attention to her - very accurate - judgments of the situation.

The light was dimmed. Maybe to hide moisture stains on carpets. Maybe in order not to liven up the hotel's customers too much and to make them go to bed quickly, instead of showing up by the bar. Or simply out of simple savings. Nina had a light at her desk, but when she turned it on, the receptionist became very visible from the outside, which did not suit her. She didn't want to attract attention. She was afraid that someone from outside would come in and hurt her. The door of the hotel was to be open until midnight. Later she could close the door, but she could keep an eye on opening it to the hotel guests in case of emergency.

The night shifts were accompanied by fear. She worked alone. It was a small hotel and the staff was kept to a minimum. Not like in the nearby big hotel, where two people worked at the reception desk on the night shift, and the bar was served until late hours by bartenders, who could be called upon to help when one of the guests started to argue. The advantage of the night shifts was a higher hourly rate of pay, little traffic, less work... And there was something else.

Something Nina had just started thinking about.

It was almost 3:00. The bar was already closed, so it was unlikely that someone would come downstairs. All the keys were issued, so nobody is likely to come. She checked the reservations. They didn't expect anyone at that time. And even if some stray guest came, well, then he will have bad luck. Let him learn to check in to the hotel at normal time. Let him sleep in the car. Or he would go to the big hotel. Nina put her shoes on swollen feet.

With a loud moaning, she got up from her chair and walked to the company's facilities. There were toilets for employees and a kitchen. And there, on the counter, there were waiting for the morning throw aways of the uneaten cakes. Maybe it will be a carrot cake?

The English liked it and it disappeared quickly, but maybe she will be lucky. The cake was flourishing all day long outside the fridge and after eight o'clock it was disappearing out of sight of the guests. It could not be sold any more, so that nobody would get food poisoning.

Nina used her cell phone to make a light. There were no CCTV cameras in the back. But she preferred to be alert. Maybe they are hidden somewhere and the employer checks if the cook spits on the meal. She knew the way to the kitchen desk by heart. She would walk around every night if she had worked. A little stress, fear that someday someone will discover her "crime"... But it was worth it. This time there was also a box on the edge of the tabletop. What are you hiding this time? Maybe some lemon cake? Maybe a better one? The box was empty. Nina unbelievably read the text placed inside.

"You're fat enough, fat enough..."

Nina, trembling with her hand, carefully put down the card to her place, to the nearest millimetre. She will not give the author any satisfaction. Let him think she hasn't read the note. She felt that the cheeks were burning. She wanted to throw the box, break a few chairs and with a kitchen cleaver chop up the office desk, then write: "I'm leaving!" with spray paint.

Unfortunately, she couldn't afford that kind of prank. She wasn't a rock star with millions of dollars in her account and she was never supposed to be one because of her poor voice.

She went to the toilet. She rinsed her face with cold water. Fortunately, in the dim light the cameras will not register the color of her cheeks. She returned to the reception desk. She stealthily looked at the CCTV camera.

Unfortunately, they were covered and it was difficult to check what they were filming at the moment. Certainly they were working automatically now, but tomorrow someone will check if she was crazy after this unpleasant surprise. She will not give them this satisfaction. She started to browse through the order papers. Unfortunately, she found an order for food. Cheesecake, chicken for "roast dinner", lasagna, pizza... Nina felt unpleasant sucking in her stomach. She took her food, but ate it before midnight.

It's three o'clock. The nearby kebab was open even until four o'clock today. Today it was a weekend and the owners were working on young people leaving numerous pubs and discos. They were delivered only until one o'clock in the morning, but she could order food, and when it was ready, walk the hundred meters and pick up, but what? pizza? kebab? But what about CCTV recording? They will see her defeat. But should she care about them? They are a bunch of ignorant fools. To be proud or to be hungry? Nina reached the phone.

'It's Nina from the hotel... Can I order a pizza? How long will it be... I'll collect it later...'

WORKAHOLIC

*T*he power's been cut all morning. As long as the batteries were on in the laptop and in the phone, it wasn't so bad. But they both ran out; the laptop died at nine o'clock in the morning and the phone was off twenty minutes later. Why the hell did I come here? I looked into my neighbour. He offered a vodka to start a relationship. I refused, excusing myself with work. That's what this stupid peasant laughed at and gave me a sermon about the fact that on Sunday nobody had made a fortune. I asked about the laptop. He said he didn't have one. I looked around looking for a car. He didn't have one either. He' s walking everywhere on his fucking feet. I got stuck here . If they don't turn on the power or repair the fault, it will be after my promotion. Julia will come to take me only in the morning. I let her choose that hour. She laughed at my foresight that something could happen and that it was better for her to come earlier. She was mocking me, so I gave up. And now I have to take care of mine. Why am I not listening to my subconscious? Or maybe it was my inner self-saboteur who spoke again? I haven't let him speak for a long time, and now please! Or maybe it was my mother-in-law's fault? Why the hell was she coming this weekend? Who normally rests in the city? And this is how she explained her arrival. I wouldn't do anything in front of her. Rest! She would speak all day that she wants grandchildren and that we should have more rest if we want to have a descendant. Rest! Rest is gone! Rest is for lazy ones! You need to be fucking busy!

I'm glad I found this paper and pen. The worst was the first hour when the phone died. Why did I try to call my boss? I should have called Julia to pick me up. The first five minutes I ended up cursing. Later I had murderous instincts, which I discharged on two spiders. Then it fell silence. There was a busy rainstorm, this one wasn't idle. I was imprisoned. I couldn't leave in my shoes. They were too expensive for the mud.

What ever tempted me to buy this lot one day? Oh, yes, it was still when I loved mountains. What did I get out of it? I screwed up my studies by riding and walking in the hills. I made it up later on, but my CV will never look perfect. If I had finished my studies later because I was working abroad, it would have made sense. But the mountains? Isn't it better to watch them in albums? I sat down and started biting my nails. Just like at work, I was fast at it too. Twenty minutes. My new record as my nails were exceptionally hard. It's been half an hour since the cell died. Later I thought I would go crazy. Nothing happened, I couldn't do anything. Fortunately, I found this paper. What to do now? Describe my project on this paper? It will not pass. It has to work and be ready for tomorrow morning.

What tempted me to work in this industry anyway? Money is a good thing to live comfortably. This is the thought I have to hold on to. Mountains will not give you happiness. Nor bread. I wonder what the neighbor is doing during such day like this one? The television probably stopped working. He got bored. Or he went to sleep. I will look out the window, maybe it will stop raining and somehow I will get to the road. There I will hitchhike and go home. Then I will finish the project. Only these shoes are a shame.

I almost had a heart attack! A neighbor sits on the stairs of his wooden cottage, smokes a pipe and seems to be satisfied. What is he happy about? As far as I know, he is a bachelor with no education and no permanent job. What does he live on? If he hadn't been so lazy, he would have done better. But for him, every day is probably Sunday and it's hard to make a profit. I'm trying to come up with an emergency plan. I should have done it earlier, but I was deceived by the world of a big city where the electricity was something obvious. I feel worse than in rehab from cigarettes. My thoughts revolve around the subject of addiction - work. What will happen if I don't show up with the ready-made software? Will the boss take me off the project? The company is full of young employees, for whom mountains are only an obstacle to overcome in the board game. The boss belongs to their group. He is ten years younger than me and there are rumours that he works for a government organization, catching gaps in their security system. I sometimes feel like a dinosaur among them. I try to keep up to date with all the latest news from our IT world, but sometimes it seems unrealistic to me. Maybe I devote too much time to Julia?

Emergency plan. My thoughts are going in wrong direction again. To go looking for electricity? Where? It is fifteen kilometres to the nearest village. In both directions it is a real expedition. Or maybe the neighbors have a generator? I went to ask and every time I had to listen to only that they do not make moonshine. Only sometimes they have a bottle for someone from the family. My shoes are all in mud. I'll take care of cleaning them, maybe they'll turn on the power at that time. I fell asleep while cleaning my shoes. On a chair, with a shoe in one and a cloth in the other hand. My nap took an hour. Maybe it was the organism that decided not to make me crazy? There is still no electricity. Water is pouring out of the sky. I feel like Julia won't be here tomorrow. I wouldn't have driven through the mud myself. Should I leave early in the morning to get to the main road? There's only one way to get here. We can't miss each other. Well, yes. It looks like I've accepted my failure. But I think the boss will understand what "force majeure" means? The best I can explain to him is a computer game. But how? Game over?

He's gonna fire me. Moving to a more difficult stage of the game? He will think that I want a raise. System error? He will say that I screwed up because instead of sitting at home and finishing the project I went to the mountains. No one goes there to work. The neighbour is still sitting outside. He smiles at his thoughts. He is dressed in an old, blue work suit, and he has a cheap, flannel checkered shirt. Only now do I notice that he is smoothly shaved and has short hair. It doesn't fit in with the whole thing. And it starts to irritate more than the lack of electricity. The latter can easily be explained, his neat appearance less. The suit is clean, the shirt is clean too. Only the rubber boots show a lot of mud. What does he do on regular days? I decided to go and destroy his good mood. Maybe he doesn't know that there is a civilization behind the mountains, that there is a kebab from a shop and not just pickles picked for moonshine? And yet he knows.

Supposedly, he goes every week to the marketplace to sell pictures. He asked if I wanted to buy it. I said I didn't like art, not wanting to have another proposal to buy a picture of a deer in the forest. I also don't like to criticize amateurs. But that smile of his well-being made me angry.

'Let me see!' I said.

'Landscape or abstraction?'

Abstraction. I imagined him splashing the canvas with a paint, supervising in the meantime the speed of making the moonshine. Of course, not on Sunday.

He brought the picture. I was overwhelmed. Not only did he know the rules of perspective, but his views looked like they were taken out of the fantasy world alive.

'Maybe it's time for a plum brandy?' He offered.

While still in shock, I nodded my head. As it turned out, the neighbor did not have any education in painting. He was self-taught. With a smile, seeing my surprise, he began to tell the story of how he dreamt of individual paintings. He had to go to work in a nearby bakery. While baking bread, he thought about every painting. When he returned home, he started to paint. Then he forgot about his tiredness, about the fact that he should eat and drink. Of course, he did not start a family because of this.

'People buy them? Is it not hard for you to give away your paintings?' I asked. 'Sometimes, when I like one, I sell a copy of it. I keep the originals at home.'

I looked at his wooden cottage.

'Not here,' he explained.

It turned out that it was his art house. Normally he lives somewhere else. I was staring like a magpie at a painting. It presented a scene from a railway station, somewhere from the beginning of the invention of steam engines.

'Do you like it?' He gave me a picture and said he would never accept money. 'But I don't even know how I'm going to pay you back' I felt a debt of gratitude to pay back.

'You gave me something more precious; your time.'

I came to my senses. The plum brandy was almost drunk. And most importantly, the light in my hut was shining. There was already a power supply.

'Yes, you don't have time for yourself,' said the peasant. 'I can see it. Go on, it must be something important.'

I came back to my hut and now I'm wondering. Do I really want to devote my whole life to a job that I don't like and that takes a dozen or so hours a day? What will I tell my grandchildren in the future? That I made sure that the return forms for a company came in the right size? After all, I always wanted to create computer games. I have just found a talented artist. And my head was full of fictional ideas. I guess it's better to say after a dozen or so years that a cult computer game has become a reality than that I earned more than the national average and could support my family? What will Julia say about this? And on what? Have I already made any decisions?

'No one's made a living on Sunday!' I mumbled to myself.

I connected the laptop and the phone to the power supply. Let them charge. And I'll rest and think about it. I didn't even have time to think. It is high time to change it.

PROMOTION

*A*fter the last rainstorm, all the poplar leaves in the alley have fallen. The intense smell of the leaves evoked a vision of a warm fireplace, hot tea, a blanket and a book in minds of most people strolling through the alley. But not with me. The inflammation of the sinuses meant that I couldn't feel most of the scents offered by nature at this time of year. I should add that in the summer I always had hay fever, so my smell didn't work well in other months. In addition to my sense of smell, I also have astigmatism, and in the evening the lanterns and street lights in my eyes were blurred like impressionist paintings. I do not wear glasses. Together with my predilection for diamond shapes' print sweaters, glasses would give me the look of a dried archivist. And that's what I was, working in the city hall. Most of the neighbors envied me for the so-called "hot job", even if they earned more than I did. "Once you get that job, you can sit there until you retire. - They reported their views on the boring work of the archivist, which in these relations took the form of a superposition.

I was wondering what causes such greed for low-paid clerical positions. Laziness?

Fear of being fired from a regular job and unemployed? Being sure that you will spend half your life in the same work, doing the same thing? - You can go crazy from such thoughts of monotony, I thought. Despite the resistance to repetition, my programme of the day was very schematic. I would get up, eat breakfast and go to work. After work I cooked dinner. Punctually at 6 p.m. I was going for a walk. Then I learnt foreign languages: English, French. Incompetently I also spoke Chinese words. After learning, I read books half an hour a day. At the very end I started to write a diary. This activity, somewhat unusual for my age, gender and position, was dictated by my writing interests. I did not plan to remain in the role of an archivist of the city hall until retirement. I wanted to write and publish a book. I had already managed to write one novel, but unfortunately it was poorly written, about which I was kindly informed by a reviewer. At first I was shocked by this opinion. However, after a year I read a random page of the novel and I had to admit that the reviewer was right.

In order to practice writing, I decided to keep a journal. I described my relationships with colleagues at work, more important events of the day, my fight against addiction - I tried to quit smoking, as well as loose reflections on philosophy, read books, historical and political events. Recently, the most frequently repeated word on the pages of my diary was a word that bounced on my ears in the office: "Promotion!" Despite pretending a contestation of this event to come, my ears picked up all the gossip. I did not bind my future with this job and the position of a senior archivist was not of great value to me, but I decided to join the rat race. The senior position looks better on my CV, and the money is also much better.

ANTONI'S DIARY

23-10-2010

"Promotions, promotions!" - I hear this word several hundred times a day. Everybody's gone crazy! They have stopped surfing the Internet and pretend to be faithful employees. Only gossip can't stop. All the staff in the department are women, except for the administrator, who would do better working as a supermodel. He would have made more money, and the situation in the department would have improved if the clerks hadn't been running every five minutes to his office under the pretext of doing some very important business. Coming back to the rumours, I know everything about their neighbours, their marital, extramarital and premarital lives. Everything is a bit distorted by the point of view of the interested parties, so it is difficult to say what is an objective truth in these relations. Anyway, does the objective truth exist? There are objective facts, but if they concern several different people, then their way of perceiving events is different because of their character, experience, etc. The truth is that if they concern several different people, then their way of perceiving events is different. Take the example of Mrs Monica, whose husband is a workaholic and goes out for a beer once a week with his colleagues.

Let's assume that a man is actually working hard and doing overtime to secure his promotion and a better future for his family. After a week, he meets a friend to proudly boast of his workaholism in the form of complaining about times when you have to work harder than others to achieve anything. Perhaps he also speaks briefly to women, passing them by at the bar. In Monica's view, the non-schematic work schedule of her husband is a threat to the survival of her marriage. It is easy to hide an affair if there are many overtime hours.

'Or is he sitting in this job for so long because he has a crush on someone?' Mrs. Monika analysed it.

And what are the objective facts when none of us, including her, knows what her husband really does?

We will never know, but for a few years the office has been assured of rumours about Monica's husband's alleged affair. She herself cares about it, flooding someone every few weeks with confessions and her doubts, which will spread around the city hall as irrefutable facts. The power of gossip is powerful. Whether her husband is having an affair or not, we can all be happy about one thing - we don't have to do overtime!

30-10-2010

In order to get a promotion, you have to be better than others or try not to let other people to get it - then it will come to us. But how to sabotage the work of other clerks? I thought about it for a long time and decided to find something that would absorb them so much that they would forget about their work. Firstly, I brought some travel agency brochures under the guise of thinking about my own holidays. They quickly disappeared from my desk. Clerks who had partners started to think about how to get their partners to finance their travel and get a holiday at the same time. The singles studied romantic photos of Venice, dreaming that they would meet their dream partner on the road. Holiday romances! What is the purpose and charm of this? Come to bed with a newly met person, and after a few days to split. A substitute for a relationship. They will probably come back blooming after such an adventure, their desire for acceptance will be satisfied. But they will still be lonely. It's better to get to know someone well on the Internet. This is where I came up with another plan to direct the thoughts of my colleagues in a direction other than promotion or work. I brought some excerpts about online dating and websites specially created to match people. I used to drop off the nets for a week, bringing in leaflets from travel agencies and printouts about online romances in alternation. I have to boast of a small success. One of the most successful female employees to be promoted has already planned her vacation. She chose Malta because of the low price of the trip and the size of the country.

'I won't get lost there for sure' she joked. 'It's not as big as Africa.'

She had long dreamed of travelling to Tunisia or Morocco, but was afraid that she would be kidnapped and taken deep into the continent to make her somebody's mistress. I enjoyed her cheerfulness and excitement about going away, while at the same time wondering whether her application for leave would reduce her chances of promotion.

01-11-2010

I've decided to go crazy. I've recalculated everything, and I know I've got a poor chance of getting promoted. But I can play tricks on other employees. I am irritated by their sudden, fake enthusiasm. All personal belongings and disorder have disappeared from the desks. Every other person bought various organizers for files, office supplies and incoming documents. Cheeky blouses were replaced by subdued colors. There is nothing more to see. Everything is covered up. The skirts have been extended by a good twenty centimetres. Such is the power of promotion! I can no longer focus on learning foreign languages. My thoughts still revolve around this subject. How to spoil their fun? Well, I've come up with the idea that I'll print leaflets about the incredible promotion on the day of the announcement about who is this lucky person and will receive fifty zlotys a month. It will cost me a few hundred zlotys, but I think I would never forgive myself if I hadn't made them a joke. You have to color your archivist's life somehow.

04-11-2010

Flyers are ready. Wouldn't anyone be tempted to buy a TV set at a third of the supermarket price? And I know they are watching. I have chosen the campaign hours for the period when our manager most often appears at work. He probably sleeps until ten o'clock because he lives next door to the office, and he shows up a half an hour later. The campaign will last for only half an hour, which is supposed to explain the low price of television sets. I informed in advertising materials that there will be only ten TV sets at this price. But for what they are! Awesome, so that a whole year's bonus from promotion wouldn't be enough for them. We will see what my colleagues will choose and what they will do with their work. I still can't learn, this time excited about my prank and imagining the possible consequences of my action. But you live only once.

―――――――――――――――

10-11-2010

Today is the day of announcing who is the chosen one. The time of the TV campaign is approaching. Employees nervously pick their nails. Did they find the leaflets? The tension is more intense than in electric cables. I couldn't stand it and decided to go out for a cigarette, politely informing my friends about it, which I always did. Although I knew they didn't notice my presence or temporary absence. This time my information caused a lament.

'Where are you going?' One screamed out. 'To get a TV?'

'I don't watch TV.'

'Yeah, well, just sit there a little longer, and we'll go for a cigarette together.'

'But you don't smoke?' I was surprised.

'What does an old bachelor know about women,' I heard in reply.

"Oh, you bitches!" - I thought. "I'd like to see your faces at the cash register in this shop." Calmed down by this thought, I sat down in my chair.

'What a loser!' I got a comment.

Five minutes later, the manager appeared in his ceremonial pink tie, which he wore only for special occasions. He also had a solemn mine, until he noticed the absence of the ladies.

'I wanted to call a meeting... But I can see that there is no one.'

'If there's no one here, who are you talking to?'

The manager cleared his throat and looked at me from an angle. I was right. This promotion wasn't for me.

'So where did our friends go?' The manager became interested.

'The TV sets were given away for 100 zlotys each, but only ten.'

'Well, that's right. I'll take a walk there. Someone has to save our dear girlfriends from the hustle and bustle of shopping, right?' He laughed. 'But what can you know about it...'

'Surely nothing' I nodded, at the same time realizing that I did the right thing, investing money in leaflets. They will never know, and I will have satisfaction.

12-11-2010

And yet they found out. I don't have a promotion. Actually, I don't even have a job. The angry manager, encouraged by the employees, gave me a small audit. During this procedure he found a forgotten invoice for the printing of leaflets.

21-11-2010

I registered with the Employment Office. I feel that a new chapter in my life is opening up. I will get my benefit and I am going to write a novel about my life during this time.

Printed in Great Britain
by Amazon

10774857R00075